The Surprise

by
GEORGE SHANNON
pictures by JOSE ARUEGO
and ARIANE DEWEY
Greenwillow Books, New York

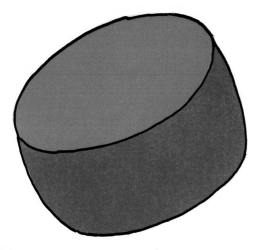

Library of Congress Cataloging in Publication Data

Shannon, George.   The surprise.
Summary: Squirrel gives his mother a
special surprise on her birthday.
[1. Birthdays—Fiction.   2. Mothers—Fiction.
3. Squirrels—Fiction.   4. Gifts—Fiction]
I. Aruego, Jose, ill.   II. Dewey, Ariane, ill.   III. Title.
PZ7.S5287Su 1983   [E]   83-1434
ISBN 0-688-02313-4
ISBN 0-688-02314-2 (lib. bdg.)

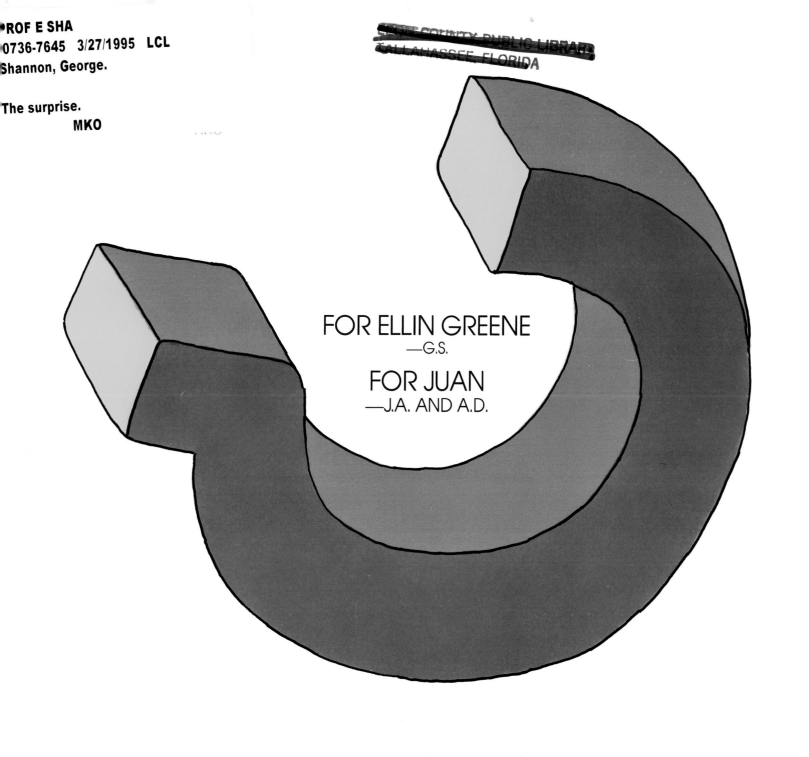

FOR ELLIN GREENE
—G.S.

FOR JUAN
—J.A. AND A.D.

Squirrel
was
worried.

His mother's birthday was one day away, and he still hadn't found her a present.

He had
looked in
all the stores
in town,
but nothing
seemed
just right.

She had
perfume and
books and the
most beautiful
garden.
He'd already
given her drawings,
and songs that
he'd made up.

And
every time
he made
a cake,

he
burned
it.

He sighed
and said,
"I'll just have
to send her
a plain old
birthday card."
But as he
was putting
the stamp on,
he had
an idea.

He called
his mother
on the telephone
and said,
"I'm sending you
a package with
a surprise inside.
Be sure to open it
right away."

The next day
when the
package arrived,
his mother took
off the ribbons
and opened
the box.

But
there
was
only
another
box
inside.

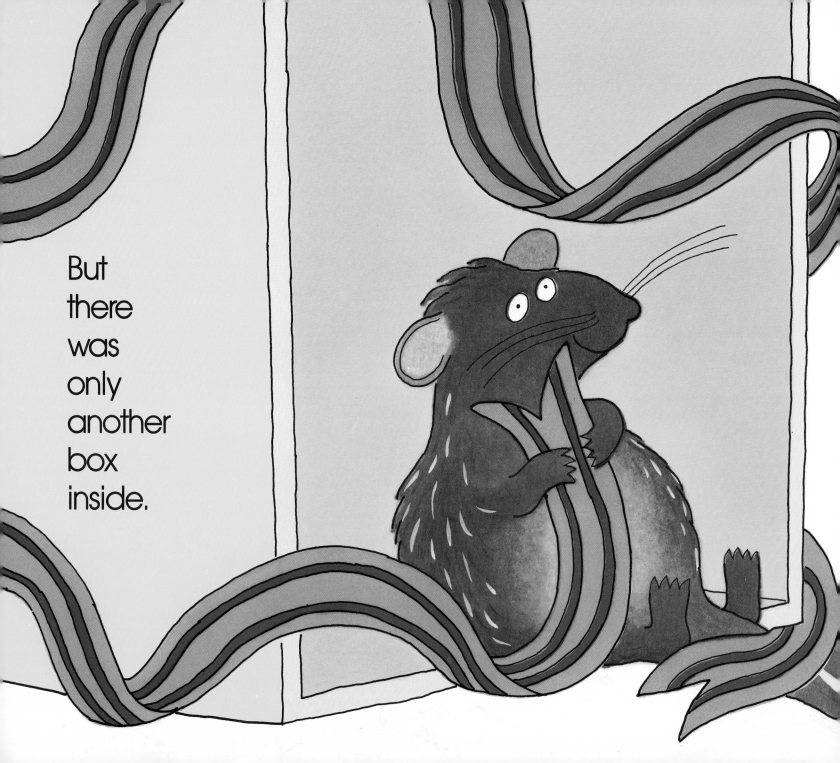

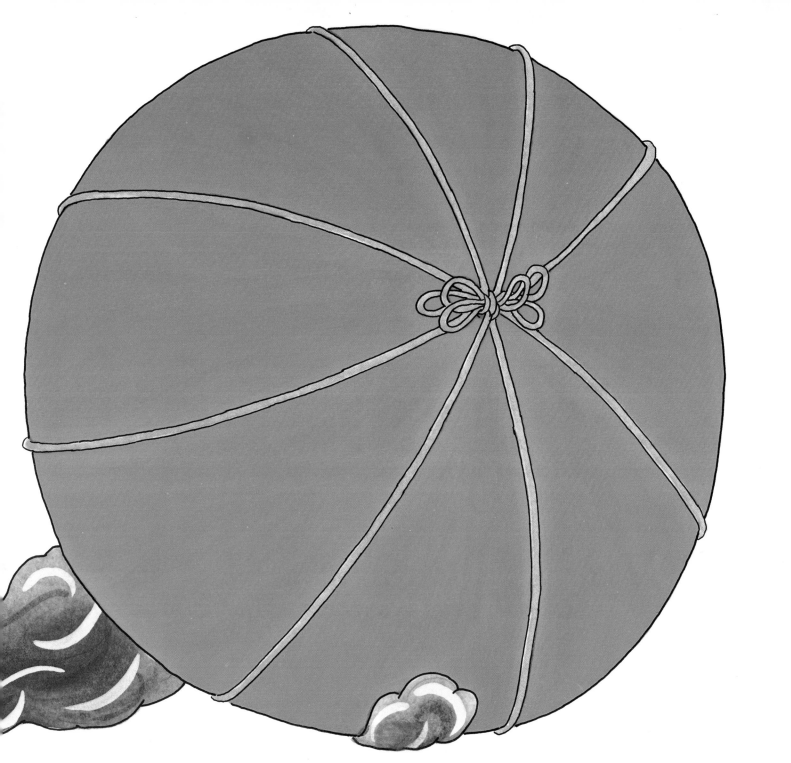

So she
opened
that box,
and
found
another
box.

And
opened
that box
and found
another
box.

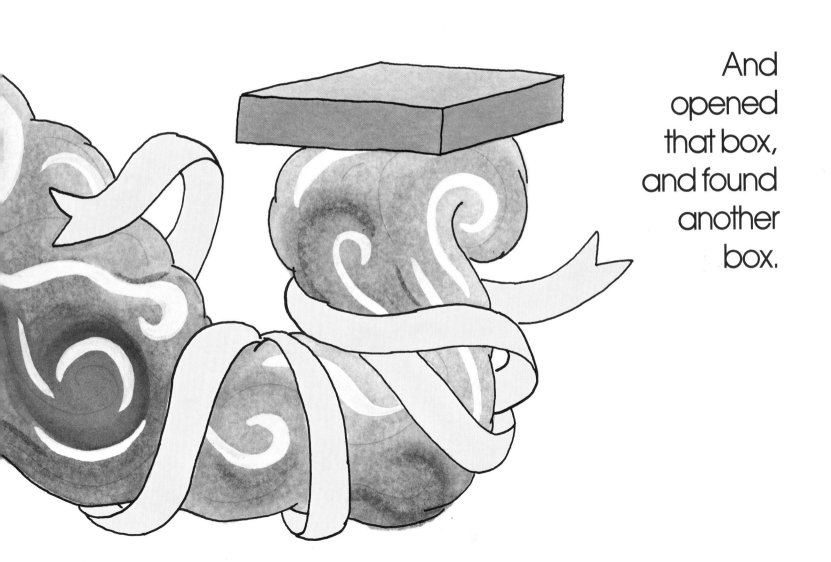

And
opened
that box,
and found
another
box.

And when
she opened
that box . . .

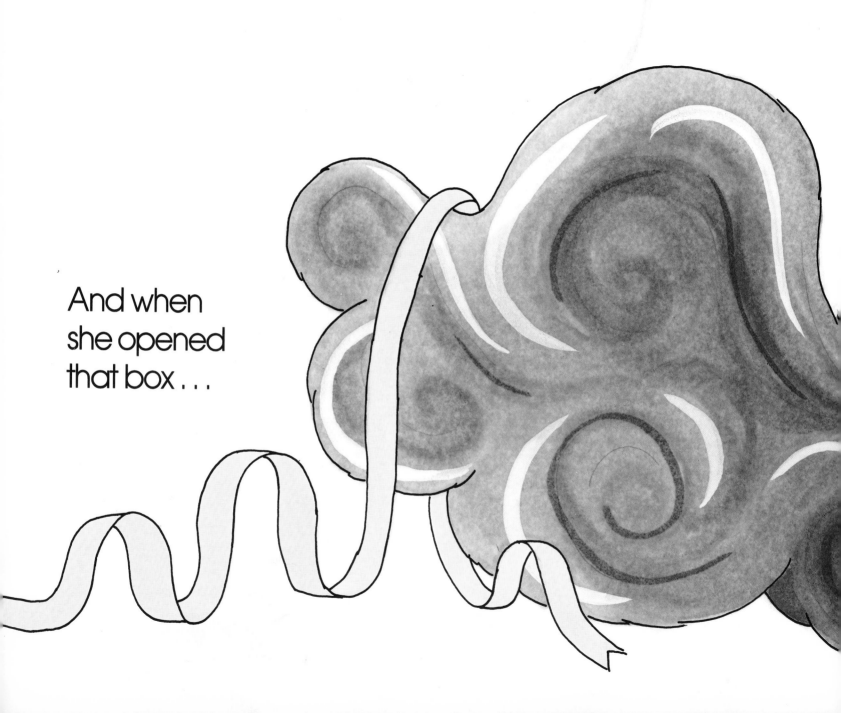

Squirrel
jumped out
and
gave her
a kiss!